Ralph Thomas

Aggravating Ladies

Ralph Thomas

Aggravating Ladies

ISBN/EAN: 9783337113933

Printed in Europe, USA, Canada, Australia, Japan

Cover: Foto ©Andreas Hilbeck / pixelio.de

More available books at **www.hansebooks.com**

AGGRAVATING LADIES

BEING

A LIST OF WORKS PUBLISHED UNDER THE PSEUDONYM OF
" A LADY," WITH PRELIMINARY SUGGESTIONS
ON THE ART OF DESCRIBING BOOKS
BIBLIOGRAPHICALLY.

BY

OLPHAR HAMST

"The time is coming when really learned men will again be ashamed of
not seeing the value of all the uses of mind : when nothing but thoughtlessness or impudence, mercurial brain or brazen forehead, will aver that
no knowledge is practical, except that which ends in the use of material
instruments." —Prof. De Morgan (Arithmetical Books 1847, p. 54).

LONDON
BERNARD QUARITCH 15 PICCADILLY
1880.

CONTENTS.

PREFACE.

In the course of collecting materials for my "Handbook of Fictitious Names of Authors of the Nineteenth Century," I came across the titles of a number of works purporting to be written by "A Lady," the authorship of which appeared to be unknown.

It occurred to me that I might probably ascertain the names of many of the authors, and also proper descriptions of such of the books as I had not seen, and was unable to see, if I printed a list of them. As however, the essential points to be attended to, in the proper description of a book, are little understood, I thought it would be desirable to prefix to the list a few suggestions on the way to supply correct information. These gradually developed, so that I soon found the subject required more space, more time, and more consideration than I at first imagined.

In the hope that I might obtain assistance from others, and with a view to getting hints and exciting discussion, I wrote an article for "Notes and Queries," which was printed in the numbers for January and April of 1872, entitled, "How to describe a Book." I now go more fully into the matters that I consider require attention in the proper description of a book.

An explanation of the title of this essay will no doubt be looked for in the preface. It is very simple. In my searches for the Authors' names, the ladies in this list have resisted all enquiry in the most aggravating manner. Therefore I took the title of Aggravating Ladies as being concise and appropriate.

The information asked for relates only to English Literature of the 19th century, to which period I confine myself entirely. The anonymous and pseudonymous writers during this century being more than sufficient to occupy a whole life of laborious application.

I have not included in the list any phrases such as :—A Lady of Rank—A Lady of Distinction —A Lady of Hebrew faith—A Banished Lady—A Young Lady—A too generous Young Lady—nor, A Lady of distinction, who has witnessed and attentively studied what is esteemed truly graceful and elegant amongst the most refined nations of Europe (!) The pseudonym of the author of The Mirror of the Graces, or an English lady's costume [treating of]...taste...grace ; modesty ...dress... ; rank...in life ;...of accomplishments ;...the mind ...means of preserving beauty... ; by a lady, &c. London, Crosby & Co., 1811.

On the other hand I have inserted some titles which have been entered in different catalogues as by "a lady," when those words do not occur on the title. Such works probably being really written by a lady, the publisher naturally desired they should go forth with that impress of good faith and with all the prestige attaching to that talismanic little word.

As I have already explained, my list comprises only works published in the present century, whose authors are unknown to me. I have a longer list of works by "a lady," whose names are known, and who have therefore ceased to be aggravating. I do not give the title when I know the name of the author because I am now seeking not supplying information.

Another list as long as that I give at the end I have not printed, not having been able to see the books themselves so as to describe them from actual inspection.

I shall be grateful for information as to any of the works, or the lives of these Aggravating Ladies.

38, Doughty Street, W.C.

July, 1880.

PRELIMINARY REMARKS.

What's in a name ?

Ask the booksellers, and they will tell you, *much* in the title-page of a new book....

The making up of a taking title-page, seems to have been the peculiar province of the bookseller, time out of mind. —*Fly leaves....London* [published and edited by] *John Miller*, 1854.

AFTER a perusal of my list I think every gentleman will agree with me that Ladies really are very aggravating. It would be curious to hear the exclamation of any lady who has written as " A lady," upon looking it over. She would probably exclaim that when she wrote as " A lady," she thought she was the only one, or at all events one of the first.

The authoress of : " How to dress on £15 a year as a lady, by a lady," would no doubt be surprised to find such a long list for the present century alone. I mention this flowing and somewhat vigorously written little work ; but it is of too recent a date for me to make any enquiry for the author's name, especially as it is a secret that, from the present popularity of the book, is not likely to be long kept. (1) For I have remarked that though these ladies do not like placing their names on their books, yet there is little desire to disguise the authorship, and enquiries are generally soon satisfied if a work has attained any success. They like to see themselves in print, so long as there is no infringement of the patent of modesty.

---

(1) Since this was written (1875) the author's name has been divulged, and there has also been a Chancery Suit in relation to the work. I have put the book in the list which follows as an illustration of some of my remarks.

The inference from this is that my list is composed chiefly
of works that have not become famous or popular, which is
the fact.   If secresy were their object, it has to the present
time been attained, for they have defied my researches.
Nevertheless I believe that to some one of the author's
friends or relations she has been known, but "no man is a
prophet in his own country," and friends and relations very
often care too little for what literary ladies are doing to
follow Captain Cuttle's advice and "make a note" of an
author's name.   Knowledge is often the greatest enemy to
the recording of facts.   People often know so well whom a
book is by, that they are not even aware of its pseudonimity.
The majority of novel readers never know the name of the
author, nor do they care to enquire, and much prefer reading
a novel "By the author of" some previous work which has
interested them.

In many cases I am asking for information which the
authoresses do not conceal, and which is well known though
unknown to me.

Thus I ascribe my not knowing the name of the author
rather to the fact of there being no one to make a note of it
when found, than any desire on the fair writer's part to re-
main unknown.   When a lady has written her first work as "a
lady" she seldom adopts that denomination in her second
work; but more frequently uses the term "By the author of"
the previous work, or " By a lady, author of," etc.

HOW TO DESCRIBE A BOOK.

"If you are troubled with a pride of accuracy, and would have it completely taken out of you, print a catalogue." (Author unknown).

Dr. Aikin used to say, that nothing is such an obstacle to the production of excellence as the power of producing what is pretty good with ease and rapidity. *The Circulator* [1825] quoted in the Manual of Laconics by John Taylor, 1838, p. 361.

Practice is the best, if not the only way to learn how to describe a book. Simply reading descriptions of what to do is of little use. Indeed practice is found to teach so much, that we often find authors of bibliographical books cancelling the early portions of their works in order to correct those defects and deficiencies which experience has brought forcibly to their notice. Such was the case with the first part of Quérard's France Littéraire, which was called in and cancelled; and the Bibliotheca Cornubiensis of Boase and Courtney, published by Longmans in 1874.

Every one must be guided by their particular requirements; but must never lose sight of the absolute necessity there is of following a system rigidly, and of being accurate.

With these preliminary remarks I will now proceed to give some hints derived from my own experience.

CATALOGUING.

"The sheet-anchor of cataloguing-work, as of all other true work that a man has to do, is accuracy."—*Edward Edwards* (Memoirs of Libraries, 1859, vol. II. 868).

. . . "l'exactitude est le meilleur fondment du succès des livres de bibliographie."—Quérard, Omissions et bévues du livre intitulé La Littérature Française contemporaine ... 1848, p. xv.

"As bibliographers, we cannot indeed but wish, that the catalogue of every library were a bibliographical dictionary of its books.... There is no species of literary labor so arduous, or which makes so extensive demands upon the learning of the author, as that of the preparation of such works."—Smithsonian Report on the construction of catalogues... By C. C. Jewett....1853, p. 10.

"It is impossible to labor successfully, without a rigid adherence to rules. Although such rules be not formally enunciated, they must exist in the mind of the cataloguer and guide him, or the result of his labors will be mortifying and unprofitable."—Ibid, p. 17.

I have used the word Bibliography, but I must warn the student that it is meaningless, or, rather, its meanings are so numerous and varied, being used for every sort of thing connected with books, that for any scientific purpose the word is useless. Bibliotheca also is used amongst other things to express a miscellaneous collection of titles; whether good, bad, or indifferent, matters little.

What is wanted is a short word which shall express that a book is accurately described. The word catalogue is worse for its indefinite meaning than bibliotheca or bibliography. The science or art of describing books has no technical term. (2)

---

(2) The reader can refer to Notes and Queries, 4 Series IX, p. 8, for some remarks on the inconvenient length of bibliographical words.

In describing books, accuracy is the one thing to attain. And the object should be so to describe the book, that anybody else shall be certain from the description that a particular book they have in hand is the one described.

So difficult did Prof. De Morgan consider this, with regard to early printed books that he said if he had to do his work on "Arithmetical Books" over again he would invariably describe some defect or error in the printing.

I now propose to give some hints on this subject, promising that there is at present no "Grammar" of Bibliography —nothing settled, no recognized authority.

Supposing a person were about to make a catalogue of a library, or even of a few books, the first thing to do is to lay down certain rules, to be strictly adhered to, or adopt rules laid down by another for that purpose. This has been done for many years past by the librarians of our National Library. So that there at least we have a Catalogue that we can depend upon so far as it goes : how far that is the rules inform us. Several of them simply provide against the prevailing loose notions of cataloguing. Rules for example to tell us that titles are written straight on as they are found, or in the language in which the book is written and not in another, read like satires on ignorance. And yet how necessary they are.

These rules, invaluable as a guide to every catalogue maker, will be found printed in the : Catalogue of printed books in the British Museum, volume 1. London, printed by order of the trustees, MDCCCXLI, in folio; the Preface is signed by the editor Sir Antonio Panizzi, and examples of the rules will be found in : A handbook for Readers at the British Museum, by Thomas Nichols, assistant in the British Museum, London, Longman, 1866, p. 51. This useful little work unfortunately has no index. A catalogue drawn up according to the rules of the Museum will be found in : " A list of the books of reference in the Reading room of the British Museum."

The rules are ninety-one in number but for small libraries where provision is not required for every language under the sun, a smaller number would be sufficient. (3)

(3.) Since the above was written a most exhaustive and useful work rendering a reference to any other almost superfluous has been published, entitled " Rules for a printed dictionary catalogue by Charles A. Cutter," forming part 11 of the Special Report on public libraries in the United States, Washington, 1876.

Whatever rules are determined upon should be printed in the catalogue, so that those who consult it may know at once whether or not they are likely to find what they want and how.

The first question that arises is the amount of title page information to be given. To abbreviate or not abbreviate becomes the difficult question. It generally resolves itself into one of expense, and abbreviated titles are determined upon.

I now therefore treat of the matter as it is, and not as it should be, for if I treated it as it should be, namely with full titles, I should have little to say.

He must have been a bold man who first began to abbreviate titles for a catalogue. It is a most unsatisfactory practice, though now having long precedent for its use. It is like cutting off a leg or an arm, the body can still go on, it is true, but it is nevertheless mutilated.

The more title page information a bibliotheca gives the greater will be its usefulness. Everything, however, is subordinate to the proper description of the book. If that is done upon certain principles and rules, the cataloguer will at least be consistent, which few of the present day are.

Every word of a title may be given and yet be inaccurate, on the other hand half the title may be left out and yet be accurate (4) though not perfect as I shall presently show.

The ordinary and most popular way of referring to or describing a book is to reverse everything and alter the title. For example, let us suppose it is stated that in 1868 Messrs. Longman published an octavo volume of 800 pages by George Brown, entitled a Treatise on the best mode of ventilation. Here everything is topsy turvy, besides being incorrectly called a treatise instead of an essay. (5) The proper title being : An historical essay on ventilation, by George Brown, London, Longman, 1868, octavo, pp. xv. 786.

Instances of this kind of thing the student will find at every turn, in every publication, periodical or otherwise.

(4.) Instead of "inaccurate" and "accurate," I had written the words "unbibliographical" and "bibliographical," but as I have already explained that word does not at present necessarily include accuracy, which word will better explain what I wish to impress on the student.

(5). Refer to the remarks of Bolton Corney "On the new general Biographical dictionary", p. 33.

Another baa practice is cutting short the title page and explaining in a note what the book is about almost in the words of the author, so that all the necessary information is given, only incorrectly instead of correctly, an example of which, taken from Lowndes, will be found in my list.

The difficulty is not to find instances of looseness in describing books, but to find instances where they are properly described. I know of few bibliothecas, English or foreign, that can be relied on.

Probably these will appear to some trivial matters. Yet what thought and anxious consideration do most authors give to the titles of their works, before they finally suit their fancy; frequently, indeed, not being satisfied with them as sent forth to the world. How has the author considered whether he will put his own name, or whether he will write under a fictitious name, or his initials, or simply call himself "A Gentleman," or designate himself by the office he holds as "A Magistrate." Then, with what difficulty has he at last settled upon a publisher, and for what a number of reasons may he have done so. And yet some ruthless barbarian, who is totally ignorant of all the trouble that has been taken, and who knows nothing of the subject, cuts down our author's title without hesitation. Or perhaps, what is still more astonishing, an author himself, although he has given the matter so much thought, will sometimes on being asked, send a list of his works, in which not a single title shall be correct, in which he will leave out all the first words, erroneously state the subject as in the book instead of as it appears on the title page: omit to say when published, whether with his own name or not; and, finally, and almost invariably, leave out the publisher's name, which cost him so much pains to decide on.

OF DIFFERENT DESCRIPTIONS
OF BOOKS.

Catalogues must have nothing to do with distinctions between celebrity and obscurity. They must aim at serving the tyro no less than the professor.—*Edward Edwards* (Memoirs of Libraries, 1859, II., p. 836).

Books may be classed under four heads, namely (1) Autonymous—(2) Polyonymous—(3) Pseudonymous, and—(4) Anonymous.

1. Autonymous, the first and most common is with the author's name either on the title-page, or if not on the title-page, signed to a preface, introduction, letter, or dedication, or in some part of the book, or at the end. Speeches though usually anonymous with regard to the reporting or editing, are frequently catalogued under the name of the speaker as autonymous.

2. Polyonymous, is with several authors' names. It is usual to enter them under the name of the first author, with cross references from the others.

3. Pseudonymous, without the author's name, but with a fictitious name or designation, thus giving some indication as to the author, though possibly a very slight one. No matter in what part of the book the pseudonym appears, the work is pseudonymous. (6)

In cataloguing, the pseudonym should no more be left out, than the author's name. If an author uses a pseudonym on the title, but gives his real name in the book, it is not pseudonymous, but must be catalogued as autonymous. In this

---

(6.) For a curious instance see the Handbook of Fictitious Names, p. 94. One who is BUT an attorney : and One who thinks for himself *i. e.* T. Truewit.

case, as in all others, the pseudonym should be given, even if the title is abbreviated. In fact the pseudonym for bibliographical purposes takes the place of the author's name. I have not space here to enumerate the different classes of pseudonyms, of which there are many varieties. (7)

4. Lastly an Anonymous book is one without the author's name, whether on the title page, or any part of the book. The word anonymous has been and still is very indiscriminately used to include pseudonymous. The cataloguer must be careful not to be betrayed into this error so fruitful of inaccuracy. This class of books has resisted the most strenuous efforts of the learned to bring it within rules, every rule for cataloguing such books requiring an exception. With anonymous works having simple titles, such as " Aggravating Ladies " (supposing a work to be published anonymously with such a title) the task is easy. Though even this example will illustrate the difficulty of the subject, for there are only two words and there are two ways of cataloguing, each having advantages. By one system it would come under " Aggravating " and by the other under " Ladies." According to the system of Audiffredi (8) and of Barbier (9)

---

(7). A list, unfortunately containing many errors, will be found at the end of " A notice of the life and works of J. M. Quérard by Olphar Hamst : London, J. R. Smith, 1867." This list is adopted by John Power in his " Handy-book about books," with all my errors and a good stock of his own to boot. There is an extended treatise on pseudonyms in the introduction to either edition of Quérard's " Supercheries Littéraires Devoilées." The subject is also treated of in M. Octave Delepierre's "Supercheries littéraires, pastiches," Londres, Trübner, 1872. Probably the earliest treatise is that entitled " Auteurs déguisez," Paris, 1690, by Adrien Baillet, but published without his name.

(8.) Audiffredi's work, referred to in the Report on the British Museum (1850, p. 469), it is entitled " Bibliothecæ Casanatensis catalogus librorum typis impressorum," tom 1—4, A—K. Roma, 1761— 1788, fol., and is quoted by Barbier at p. xlviii of the work referred to in the next note.

(9.) Dictionnaire des ouvrages anonymes et pseudonymes.... par A. A. Barbier... Paris, 1806, 4 vols, 8o. It is curious to note that Barbier had not settled in his own mind at the date of the above the first edition, what was an anonymous work. He describes it as one upon the title page of which the author is not named, and he then states that sometimes the author's name is found in the work; but he says it is the custom to class them all as anonymous and not to distinguish different degrees of anonymity. In the second edition in 1826 he very properly eliminated so far as he was able such works as contained the authors' names. For many things the first edition

and of a similar work on English authors (10), it would be catalogued by the first word, and for such works this is the most approved method (11). According to the Rules of the British Museum it would be catalogued under Ladies.

It affords matter for consideration when we find it stated that " An anonymous work is seldom read with confidence or quoted as an authority." (12)

Many publications intended expressly for youth, and therefore requiring some guarantee that they are fit for the purpose, are published without the author's name, though frequently with an indication of sex.

It may probably be that little as is the credit given to the anonymous or pseudonymous work, for in the above quotation both are meant, it would obtain less if it had the author's real name (13).

To shew that a book was published without the author's name, whether anonymous or pseudonymous, some bibliographers have put an asterisk or star at the beginning of the title. I am not aware that this, or indeed any plan has systematically been adopted in any English work, except within the last few years. In his learned Essay On the Literature of Political economy, p. x, J. R. McCulloch says : " When the name of the author of a work is included between brackets, it shows that it was published anonymously." He

---

is better than the second, in which many of the titles we are told were abbreviated. In the third and last and best edition, part of which was published in 1872, his son, (see p. xxix., note) has so far as he was able, re-instated such titles because so many editors and others still continue to consider a work anonymous if the author's name does not occur on the title page.   This is a step backwards, and the sooner M. Olivier Barbier throws the editors and others overboard the better.

(10.) A prospectus was issued in 1872, with the title : A dictionary of the anonymous and pseudonymous literature of Great Britain by the late Samuel Halkett.—See Notes and Queries 4 s. IX., p. 403.

(11.) And is recommended in a pamphlet entitled : Hints on the formation of small libraries, by W. E. A. Axon, London, Trübner [1869] reprinted in : A handy book about books, by J. Power, Lond., J. Wilson, 1870, p. 156, and he adopts it in : The literature of the Lancashire dialect, a bibliographical essay, by W. E. A. Axon, 1870.

(12.) Bolton Corney "On the new general Biographical dictionary," 1839, p. 15.

(13.) For examples see Notes and Queries 3rd s. XII, 394, and the Handbook of Fictitious Names.

uses anonymous here in the sense of without the author's name, and to include pseudonymous. I made use of the star in the Handbook of Fictitious Names in 1868, but only to indicate anonymity, and not as Quérard uses it. In Notes and Queries for the 6th April, 1872, I suggested the adoption of a line — to shew that a book was published pseudonymously. And I made use of both signs in my Bibliographical list of Lord Brougham's publications. These signs have the advantage of attracting the eye, and declaring at once the class of book. On the other hand they cannot be used for foot notes, are likely to be overlooked in printing, and there is always great difficulty in getting readers to find out what signs mean. On the whole after much consideration I have determined for the future to use simply abbreviations of the words anonymous and pseudonymous which everybody understands without explanation.

As in describing a book the principal object is to enable the student to identify it, so that there may be no doubt that the cataloguer's remarks upon a certain book apply to that for which the reader is searching. It is less important that autonymous works should be catalogued so fully as anonymous, because the author's name is at once a guide. For though two autonymous works bear the same title their authors' names would be different. But not so with two anonymous works having the same title.

Pseudonymous works, in which the pseudonym is a name and not a phrase or denomination, would come in the same category.

For anonymous, and frequently for pseudonymous works it is not only desirable to give the full title, but to supplement it with any further information that will help identification. As for example, if the book is printed at a different place to that of sale or publication (14) or if dated and addressed from what would appear to be the author's residence, or if there is any allusion in the work or the advertisements (15) to other publications of the same author. Examples of

---

(14.) Many London publishers have printing houses out of town, in such cases the place of printing is no guide.

(15.) Advertisements should generally be preserved. If, however, a book has been through a binder's hands there is little chance of their surviving. Never send a book to the binder without special instructions to preserve the advertisements and covers or wrappers, and

all will be found in my list.   Though a book be anonymous so far as the title page informs us, yet if pseudonymous from the preface or introduction being signed with a fictitious name, or with initials or denomination, or other qualification, it should be catalogued as pseudonymous.   Thus following the rule with regard to antonyms.   Except when signed :— The Author, The Editor, The Translator, Himself, or Herself, of which it is best to take no notice, even if on the title. Such works should be considered anonymous without even giving cross-references from those words.

Of whatever description, whether antonymous, or anonymous, or pseudonymous, the first words of the title, or the half title, should be quoted correctly, and exactly as they occur, and to this rule there should be no exception, whether for bibliographical lists, or for the purpose of citation as an authority.   For in the latter case, however familiar the work cited may be, there are sure to be readers unfamiliar with it, to whom a loose reference will cause trouble.   The half title or any abbreviation of the title, if used by the author of the book may be adopted.

Few things cause greater waste of time amongst literary men than the habitually careless manner in which they give references.   Not only should a book be correctly described, but the edition or date and page ought to be added.   Bibliographers (which term I here use to mean persons who have concerned themselves with the description of books) have sinned terribly in this respect by giving descriptions of books at second, or even third-hand, and repeating the mistakes and blunders of the original authority.   Title pages are like rumours, the oftener they are repeated the more incorrect they become.   The student should never rely upon a catalogue for the description of a book, unless the compiler has adhered strictly to rules.   A statement in bibliothecas, biographical dictionaries, or catalogues, that a work is anonymous, can never be relied upon (16).

---

mark every page intended to be kept, otherwise there is a barbarous custom amongst binders, arising from ignorance or cupidity, of denuding every pamphlet of the covers and advertisements which frequently teem with matter useful in after years.   Binders like to treat books like convicts, and shave their heads.

(16.) Those who desire to see examples of several classes of errors to be avoided can refer to the following works.   On the new general Biographical dictionary : a specimen of amateur criticism in letters [signed Bolton Corney] to Mr. Sylvanus Urban [motto] London: Sho-

After the first few words of the title every abbreviation or omission should be indicated by three dots ... close together not thus. . . . This is a better method than using an "etc.," a sign which from the carelessness of authors is frequently found on title-pages of books, and if used by both authors and cataloguers we should never know which. As few authors could explain the meaning of an " &c." on the title, it is not likely that readers can guess.

It has been customary to omit mottoes without any indication of the omission, and this has been done in one of the most bibliographical works published in England (17). I only know of one work of importance where special notice is taken of such omissions. (18)

If a title page has a motto its omission should be shewn thus [motto].

To print mottoes when numerous or lengthy in an extensive work seems quite out of the question. When short it

---

berl, 1839, 8o. A remarkable piece of criticism indispensable to every biographer or bibliographer.

Arithmetical books....being brief notices of a large number of works drawn up from actual inspection by Augustus de Morgan.... London, 1847. See the preface and introduction to this valuable and interesting work. The English catalogue of books, 1864, makes an edition of this work with the date 1853, at 2s 6d. Being desirous of possessing this, I wrote to the learned Professor to know where it was to be obtained, and what difference there was, he replied :—"The difference between the 1st and 2nd edition of my Arithmetical Books, is the difference between something and nothing, which, let Hegel say what he will, is a very great difference. There is not any second edition, nor I think, will be." Refer also to an article by De Morgan in the Companion to the Almanac for 1853, entitled "On the difficulty of correct description of books," pp. 5 to 19, full of various and useful matter.

Handbook of Fictitious names of authors of the XIXth Century.... by Olphar Hamst..., 1868, p. xi.

Dictionnaire des ouvrages anonymes par A. A. Barbier, 3e. ed., 1872, see the note by Olivier Barbier on the second page of the advertisement to the first volume.

(17.) A descriptive catalogue of Friends' books, ... by Joseph Smith, in two vols, ... 1867.

(18.) This is the: Catalogue of the Manchester free library, reference department, prepared by A. Crestadoro, ... 1864, where the omission is indicated by three stars.

In my " List of works on Swimming," I give full titles, including mottoes of all the books I was able to see. In my " Bibliographical list of Lord Brougham's publications," I indicate the place of the motto on the title.

is a luxury the bibliographer may occasionally indulge in. I confess that this is one of the points I have felt extremely puzzled about.   I never abbreviate or omit anything from a title-page without fear and trembling, which is intensified in the case of mottoes.   They frequently in one short verse, or sentence, give the pith of a book, and my fear is that some one in the future should wonder how I could be so stupid as to suggest their omission.

All additions should be indicated with the same care by placing them between brackets [   ].   Additions in titles should be as few and as short as possible, all explanatory matter can be given in a note.

Sometimes authors use brackets or parentheses on the title pages.   When this is the case, if of no use or unimportant, they should be left out by the cataloguer.   For instance, when an author has the words [Reprinted from, &c.] in the title.   To omit the brackets is the least misleading, for if left in it would look as if this information were not supplied by the author, and if (*sic*) were put it would not be understood as referring to the brackets.

MATTERS TO BE ATTENDED TO IN CATALOGUING.

In arranging a number of rules, it is difficult to please every reader. I have frequently been unable to satisfy myself; and therefore, cannot expect that the arrangement which I have at last adopted will give universal satisfaction.— W.LENNIE, The principles of English grammar...34th ed., Edinb., 1854, p. 4.

Cataloguers may comment upon, but should never alter what it has been deemed right to state on the title page of a book by those who have framed it.—Art of making catalogues, &c.[by A. Crestadoro], 1856, p. 14.

In cataloguing or describing a book six points at least should be kept in view as necessary to its identification. (19)

(1.) Title.
(2.) Name of author, and sometimes description.
(3.) Place of publication.
(4.) Publisher's name, and sometimes address.
(5.) The date of publication.
(6.) The size.

If full titles (that is, an exact transcript of the title from beginning to the end), are given, it will only be necessary for the cataloguer to supply in its proper, or most suitable place, such of the above information as is not on the title-page.

If abbreviations be adopted several considerations arise.

(I.) As to so much of the title as occurs before the author's name we have already said that the first few words should

---

(19.) The student may refer to the useful little pamphlet above quoted, entitled : The art of making catalogues of libraries, or a method to obtain in a short time, a most perfect, complete, and satisfactory printed catalogue of the British Museum library, by a reader therein [Dr. Crestadoro], Lond. 1856, p. 38.

be copied word for word, and afterwards every omission should be denoted by dots.

(2.) The name of the author should not be abbreviated, if it renders it difficult to distinguish between two with the same initials. If the author's qualifications are omitted or abbreviated, dots ... of omission should be inserted. A description after a name is often very important and useful in determining the degree of credit to be attached to the work, but they are frequently so numerous that they are too long for most catalogues.

Works in more than one volume generally have the number on the title, as " In three volumes, vol 1." Take no notice of " Vol I.," but invariably state the number of volumes in the order in which it occurs on the title-page. The number of volumes, however, is not always stated; in some works each volume simply has " Vol I," or " Vol II," on the title, when this is so, the number of volumes should be stated after the date thus : " 1873, in three volumes, octavo." The reader would then know whether the number of volumes was stated on the title or not.

There will be cases where this rule will not sufficiently indicate the fact, as for instance, when the first does not, but the second does, state the number of volumes. A note will meet this case, if necessary.

It may appear to some that so trifling a matter is unworthy of note, but with this the cataloguer has nothing to do. His business is to note facts however trivial, whether anybody should ever require them is not in his province.

(3.) Place of publication. Several places of publication are frequently given in the imprint of a book, when this is the case, the first place should, at all events, be given, and if the book is not printed as well as published there, the place where it is printed should be stated.

(4.) The Publisher's name we seldom find in any list of books. I never recollect to have seen it in any catalogue of a library, and in very few bibliographical works. And yet it is often of great importance. In cataloguing works without the author's name it should seldom if ever be omitted, however much the title is abbreviated. The publisher's address may often be added with advantage, especially in cases where he is little known. For many firms who have been issuing works from the same house for a century or even longer, it seems superfluous. (20)

(20.) I must remind the student that I am only writing for present century books, I have no experience of cataloguing old books.

Both name and address of publishers may be abbreviated without marks of omission, a rule having been made to that effect, so that the reader may be apprised of the fact. Some small elementary works have as many as ten or fifteen places and double that number of publishers in the imprint, these of course would not be given in full unless with some special object.

The publisher's name when well known is also important as frequently giving a character, or guarantee, if not of the literary worth of a book, at all events of its sincerity.

If the publisher is also the author, but does not signify that fact, the book must be considered anonymous. The publisher's name (that is the author's) must be repeated, as would be the case if written by another person.

Privately printed (21) works are frequently issued without the name of a publisher or bookseller, though less frequently without that of a printer, which if not on the title should be supplied in parenthesis or in a note.

(5.) The date of publication, if not on the title, will like the author's name, be frequently found in some other part of the book. It should then be supplied after the last word on the title in parenthesis. If not in the book, it should be put between brackets [   ], and if uncertain with a note of interrogation.

Stereotyped books are generally without dates of publication for certain commercial reasons. Only superficial readers are duped by the artifice, for the first object of the literary student would be to determine approximately the date of issue. When the preface is not dated it is no doubt as often through thoughtlessness as intention.

In quoting a work that has passed through numerous editions, it is often useful to give the date of the first.

There is a practice amongst publishers of post dating books issued towards the end of a year. (22) This practice will account for the dates of books in some bibliothecas, biographies and catalogues, sometimes being a year earlier than

---

(21.) For examples the student can refer to the only English work on the subject, of which two editions have been issued, viz., Martin's Bibliographical catalogue of privately printed books. It is necessary to have both editions in consequence of the death of the author, unfortunately interrupting the completion of the second.

(22.) See the article referred to (p. 19) by Prof. De Morgan, in the Companion to the Almanac.

the date on the book. The title having been copied from an advertisement or a review of the work apparently before publication. When known to the cataloguer the actual year of issue should be supplied in brackets immediately after the date of the title.

(6.) With the different descriptions of sizes of books Professor De Morgan was so exasperated that after giving descriptions of how the sheets of a book are folded he says, "The words *folio, quarto, octavo, duodecimo, decimo-octavo*, refer (in his book) entirely to size, as completely as in a modern sale catalogue, the maker of which never looks at the inside of a book to tell its form. All the very modern distinctions of *imperial, royal, crown, atlas, demy*, &c., &c., &c., I have relinquished to paper-makers and publishers, who alone are able to understand them." (23)

All the words in use to describe sizes are useless. They convey no definite idea to the reader, for the simple reason that nothing definite as to size is meant. The only definite meaning is that the paper is folded into certain divisions, and not that the paper or print is of a particular size. A quarto is often the size of an octavo, and an octavo the size of a quarto, duodecimo, or anything else. Nevertheless though not certain, the terms do in most cases, enable us to guess at the probable or approximate size. The only way to be certain of the size is to state it in inches. (24) Probably few literary men would put up with the trouble of measuring.

Compilers of Catalogues of modern books may content themselves in most cases with the terms at present in use. (25)

Novels are generally described in the advertisements as

(23.) Arithmetical Books, p. xii.

(24.) This plan is advocated in a work I cannot too strongly recommend. It is indispensable to every librarian. The learned author thoroughly studied all the various systems in vogue, and founds almost a code for the cataloguer upon them. It is the :—Smithsonian Report on the construction of catalogues of libraries and their publication by means of separate stereotyped titles, with rules and examples, by Charles C. Jewett, Librarian of the Smithsonian Institution, second edition. Washington, published by the Smithsonian Institution, 1853, 8vo, pp. xii., 96. Since the above was written Mr. Cutter's Rules have appeared (see p. 11), and should be referred to.

(25.) For what these are, and how to know them, I must refer the reader to the Smithsonian Report, previously quoted, or to a note by Charles Naylor on "the size of a book" in Notes and Queries for 10 Feb., 1872, 4th s., ix. p. 122.

" post octavo," which is not octavo at all, but duodecimo. The mis-description is of little importance, for everybody knows about the size of the modern three volume novel, a little larger now than at the beginning of the century.

It is annoying that so small a matter as the size of a book should occupy so much space. It has always been a subject of difficulty. A bookseller as such, in his sale catalogues, will describe a book as 12mo, but when he compiles a bibliographical list he will describe it correctly as octavo, though the actual size is what is looked upon as duodecimo.

These points are strictly necessary for ordinary catalogues, but they will not satisfy all enquiries, for we cannot tell from them whether it is a book or a pamphlet that is described. It is therefore desirable to add the number of pages. In the paging we have as much variety as in the sizes, authors, publishers, and printers, not having the slightest thought for bibliographers, and the infinite trouble of collation.

A book should be paged in as simple a manner as possible. This is a rule that has never been attended to, and so long as authors do not know their own minds never can be. If the printer begins the paging regularly, and the author thinks irregularly, and recollects something that has been left out, irregular paging will be the result. (26)

Always count from the very first printed page belonging to the book, excluding advertisements. Give the paging as printed, that is, in the same characters. If leaves occur unpaged, either before those paged or after, use arabian numerals to denote those unpaged.

(26.) The most disorderly book I know in this respect is:—" A universal alphabet grammar and language, ... by George Edmonds,... [1856] quarto :—The following is the collation. Its length would generally preclude its being given in a bibliotheca. First we have the preface vii pages, then a table of contents vii pages ; the introduction 34 pages, a half-title unpaged, then 152 pages, then another half-title unpaged, then pp. 44 and iii., then corrigenda pp. ix., then a half-title and " the Dictionary," forming a third of the book entirely unpaged. then the addenda paged separately pp. 3. Sometimes the figures of paging are at the side, sometimes in the middle, sometimes at the top and sometimes at the bottom ! Timperley in his "Printer's Manual " (1838) p. 18, says, " Running titles may be set to an index, but folios are seldom put unless with a view to recommend the book for its extraordinary number of pages ; for as an index does not refer to its own matter by figures, they are needless in this case." When the trouble that a variety of pagings gives the bibliographer, is considered, it is to be hoped that the simplicity I recommend will be adopted as much as possible.

Sometimes an octavo book begins with, say xii. numbered pages and then occur four unnumbered, and then we have page 1 on signature B, numbered consecutively to page 253, and three pages of appendix and errata beyond. Describe it thus: octavo pp. xii., and 4, and 253, and 3. But if 4 and 3 are numbered with roman numerals, it should be thus :— octavo, pp. xii., and iv., 253, iii., because this is more accurate. We use the same kind of numerals used in the book. It is, however, not a matter of much moment, provided the correct number of pages is given in the collation.

I do not use the sign plus (xii.+iv.+iii.) because it makes the figures look more uninteresting, and signs enough occur in the titles themselves.

The price at which a book is published is often unascertainable, and it is useful to insert it, though it has nothing to do with its literary or scientific value. But in this as in every other particular it is impossible to say what the student may require, and its omission might make a man of genius waste precious hours which it is the special object of the true bibliographer to save.

If the price is mentioned on the title page, accuracy requires that it be given in its regular order, whether at the beginning or end of the title. Instances will be found in the list of works by a lady at the end.

STYLE OF PRINTING.

I now come to a few minor points of printing, for in a catalogue nothing is so trivial as not to require attention.

In the previous observations I have treated of things that are invariable, they must be attended to, in any list of books, there is no room for exercise of taste, they go to the very root of a good catalogue, and are laws dictated by accuracy.

But the manner in which a title is printed in a list or catalogue, or biography is a matter of taste, and we therefore give the following hints merely as suggestions (27), hoping that they will commend themselves to all who print title-pages. Have as few capitals as possible in the title, none except for names of persons or places. Titles of persons may well be printed without capitals, as prince, marquess, lord, not Prince, Marquess, Lord.

Take for example the following title, which, printed according to the usual method would be :—

"Speeches by the Lord Chancellor; Lord Brougham, Lord Cottenham; and Lord Campbell, in The House of Lords, on Tuesday the 9th, August, 1842, at giving Judgment in the Appeal, the Rev. John Ferguson and others, Appellants, against the Earl of Kinnoull, and the Rev. R. Young, Respondents, with the Judgments appended, from Mr. Gurney's Shorthand notes," &c.

(27.) Most of which have been acted on, if not carried to their fullest extent in my study, already referred to : "A bibliographical list of lord Brougham's publications," printed in Lord Brougham's Works, ... Edinb., A. and C. Black, 1873, vol XI., pp. 463 to 486.

I prefer this title-page for catalogue purposes to be printed thus :

Speeches by the lord chancellor [Lyndhurst], lord Brougham, lord Cottenham, and lord Campbell in the house of lords, on tuesday the 9th august, 1842, at giving judgment in the appeal, the rev. John Ferguson and others, appellants, against the earl of Kinnoull and the rev. R. Young, respondents ; with the judgment appended from Mr. Gurney's shorthand notes. Edinb. James Gall and son [1842], 8o, pp. 36, 1s. The improvement in appearance of this title and the facility in reading, counterbalance all such objections as that we are accustomed to Lord, and not lord, or Tuesday, and not tuesday. The compilers of the [English] Law List have long since discarded capitals for the names of streets with great advantage, for example they print, " gray's-inn-square," not Gray's Inn Square : " court of exchequer "; "house of lords," &c. The Catalogue of the Advocates library, lately printed, is a good example ; refer for instance to the title under Bullion, vol I., 1867, p. 763, a title that in ordinary catalogues would bristle with capitals.

PUNCTUATION.

THE punctuation should also be carefully considered. Everything in bibliography is at present very much over punctuated, half, if not two thirds, might be dispensed with to the lessening of the expense, and the great advantage in the appearance.

Imagine you are copying a sentence instead of a title page, and punctuate and put capitals accordingly. If writing that a work was by an author, nobody would write By, neither need it have a capital for a copy of a title.

Mr. Henry Stevens has advocated and adopted this method in his later catalogues and notably in the :— "Bibliotheca geographica and historica or a catalogue of a nine days sale of rare & valuable ... books... et cetera ... with an essay upon the Stevens system of photobibliography by Henry Stevens GMB [*i.e.* gatherer of musty books] ... [with a photograph of] Ptolemy's World by Mercator 1578 Part I. to be dispersed by auction by Messrs Puttick and Simpson ... London Henry Stevens at the Nuggetory 4 Trafalgar square July 25 1872."

The title, which I have abbreviated nearly one third, has upwards of two hundred words in it without a single mark of punctuation, except after "Part I." where it seems to have got in by accident. Throughout his titles, he uses stops very sparingly. Any word which is complete requires no stop. Thus : "vols" requires no stop after it, because it is a finished abbreviation, but vol. does (28).

(28.) Mr. Stevens' work contains an essay on catalogues, teeming with useful suggestions, as indeed might be expected from one who has had such long and varied experience.

THE BEGINNING AND THE END.

> The unwise seem to be of opinion that any fool can index,
> but we have already seen that the wise think differently.
> —Wheatley's What is an index? 1879, p. 41.

THE beginning of every book should be a table of contents,
or an analytical table, or both, and the end a good index.

I can scarcely over estimate the importance which I
attach to the index. A book may almost as well be unwrit-
ten, as be without an index.

The publications by "a lady," are exceedingly deficient
in indexes. It is amazing that authors who must have felt
the want of indexes in the works of others should publish
their own without such helps.

It would occupy too much space to give all the opinions
I have collected of different authors entreating others never
to publish a book without an index. Allibone never loses
an opportunity, in his Dictionary of English Literature, of
impressing upon his readers the importance of indexes. See
more particularly an article of absorbing interest under the
name of Samuel Ayscough of the British Museum, celebrated
for his most useful indexes to Shakespeare, to that grand store-
house of information "The Gentleman's Magazine" (obit.
1808), to "the Monthly Review," and other works. Of such
importance indeed does Allibone consider indexes, that, not
content with insisting on them throughout his three ponde-
rous volumes, he, on the very last page, gives a note "Con-
cerning Indexes." Often a good index obtains for a book a
prominent position it might not otherwise obtain; as, for
example, Godfrey Higgins's "Anacalypsis," which is said to
be in the reading room of the British Museum, from its con-

taining (29) "thousands of statements cited from all quarters, and very well indexed." What would Watt's Bibliotheca Britannica be without its two volumes of index to two volumes of authors. Bibliographical and biographical works beyond everything require the most minute indexes.

Formerly I was in love with the scientific look of a number of indexes, but I am now convinced that two heads are not better than one in this case and that one index is more useful than two. A person who consults an index wants to find something as quickly as possible, if there is only one index he cannot consult the wrong one first.

It has been suggested by Prof. De Morgan that historians by having no indexes, think to oblige their readers to go through their works from beginning to end. The contrary being the result.

If book buyers made a rule of not buying a book without an index, authors and publishers would then supply that want.

Beware, however, of snares, for such there are in this as in all else, big books with lean, lankey, and starved indexes.

Since the above was written the " Index Society " has come into existence, and published an indispensable little work, entirely devoted to this subject entitled : What is an index ? a few notes on indexes and indexers by Henry B. Wheatley...[motto] London, Longmans 1879. Besides being useful this is a most amusing book.

(29.) Athenæum, 2 Aug. 1856, p. 953, quoted by Allibone in his Dictionary, p. 843. See also p. 3140, and refer also to Ayscough, Mary Cowden Clarke, Godfrey Higgins, John Nichols, and other articles in Allibone and to his Alphabetical Index to the New Testament, Phil. [1868], published under his initials only.

OF ERRORS.

What still remains to be taken notice of are the *errata's*,...
Sometimes they are put by themselves on the even side of
a leaf, so as to face the title. But though this is very
seldom done, it is a pity that it should ever have come into
the thoughts of anyone to do it at all; for it is a maxim
to bring errata's into as narrow a compass as we con-
veniently can, and to put them in a place where they
can make no great show : since it is not to the credit
of a book, to find a catalogue of its faults annexed. It
is therefore wrong policy in those who make errata's
appear numerous and parading, in hopes of being thought
very careful and accurate ; when they only serve to witness
an author's inattention at a time when he should have
been of the opposite inclination. But the subterfuges
that are used by writers upon this occasion, are com-
monly levelled at the printer, to make him the author
of all that is amiss; whereas they ought to ascribe it to
themselves:...whoever has any ideas of printing, must con-
sequently know that it is impossible to practice that art
without committing errors ; and that it is the province
of an author to rectify them. For these several reasons
it will appear how material it is not to make an erra-
tum of every trifling fault. ... —John Smith's Printer's
grammar. 1755, quoted in Timperley's Printer's Manual,
1838, p. 19.

Le nouvel *Errata*, je le répète, est long, d'une longueur
inaccoutumée. Les auteurs semblent avoir honte d'avouer
les fautes qu'ils ont commises, ou qu'on commet pour
eux ; je n'ai pas cette pudeur menteuse ; je confesse les
fautes de mon livre.—A. JAL : préface de la seconde édi-
tion du Dict. Crit. de Biographie et d'histoire, 1872.

IT is next to impossible to avoid errors, more especially in
bibliographical works, with numbers of names and figures.
All that can be done to avoid them, of course, should be ;
but with the most minute and constant supervision errors
will creep in and oversights occur.

This, however, is no reason for adopting eccentricities. For example, Professor De Morgan in his "Arithmetical Books," adopted the singular plan of giving the dates twice, in figures and in words, the latter being abbreviated, and after all, as he himself shows, he was still liable to commit the very errors he desired to provide against.

His plan never has been, and I hope, never will be adopted by any one else. It is original, but highly inconvenient and unbibliographical in the extreme. It is to be hoped that if a new edition is ever published we shall have proper title page information in a proper manner, and be spared such eccentricities as beginning the title-page from the bottom instead of the top.

I may here remark that the learned Professor went upon the right principle, he excluded no book on the ground of unimportance, or worthlessness. He described no book unless he had seen it, which was also J. R. McCulloch's plan in his "Literature of Political Economy" (1845), but he unfortunately described only select works, without even giving a brief list of what he considered rubbish, simply saying, "We have proceeded on a principle of selection; and neglecting the others, have, with exceptions, noticed those works only which appear to have contributed to develop sound principles, or to facilitate their adoption." The consequence is if we find a book unmentioned by him, it at once becomes a question whether he excluded it because it was worthless, or because he had not seen it.

There is a large class of errors arising from the habit of one writer copying another, instead of each going to original sources.

The errors prevalent in biography and bibliography were pointed out by Mr. Bolton Corney years ago. I think it is unnecessary for me to give here any further criticisms on the method which should be pursued. The student who wishes to go deeper into the subject can refer to Bolton Corney's pamphlet: "On the New General Biographical Dictionary," already noticed.

The work I have quoted above by M. Jal is a large volume consisting almost entirely of articles in correction of those existing in other works.

No statement of any former writer should be taken for granted, if there is any more original source. Compilers of Dictionaries sin greatly in this respect. The reason is probably that to be correct requires so much time and research

c

that it does not pay to be accurate if much time is consumed.

The safest way to avoid errors would be to compare the proof of every title page with the book itself, but the labour would be enormous, and I doubt if it is practicable in most cases. Nevertheless, it is the surest way. At the same time I would not discourage anybody from attempting a catalogue or bibliotheca, although nobody can expect to do anything of much value without accuracy, the greater the accuracy the greater the value.

Nothing is satisfactory but actual inspection of the books themselves. We have quite enough of descriptions of books at second, third, or fourth hand, in nearly all existing works, and it is time now to go upon "a new and improved principle." Mr. W. Carew Hazlitt in the preface to his "Collections and Notes," 1876, has some interesting remarks on this subject to which the student can refer.

ON THE MEANS OF IDENTIFYING THE AUTHORS OF ANONYMOUS AND PSEUDONYMOUS PUBLICATIONS.

It constantly happens that "a lady," in one of her later publications will mention a former one. In this case it is necessary to look at the publication so referred to, when it will be ascertained if it is anonymous. Works are also advertised at the end of others, either as published, or forth-coming, and these works themselves must all be looked at.

A most extensive library is requisite for references such as these. Indeed, it frequently happens that the works required cannot be found even in the enormous library of the British Museum.

To take the following as an example, in Mrs. H. Mozley's : Louisa, or the bride, by the author of the fairy bower [motto]. London, James Burns, Portman street, and Henry Mozley & sons, Derby, 1842, 12o, pp. 302.

It is pseudonymous. We find advertised at the end by the same author : Bessie Gray, or the dull child. Hymns for children on the Lord's Prayer, our duty to God and scripture history. Robert Marshall, or the cleverest boy in the school. The Stanley Ghost. The old Bridge. Some published, others in the press, none of them, however, have I (1872), been able to find in the Catalogue of the Library of the British Museum (30). They may be there nevertheless.

As another example, I have traced the following works to the same author, without, however, ascertaining the author's name.

Spain yesterday and to-day, by a lady, London, Harvey and Darton [1829 ?], sm. 8o.—Portugal, or the young tra-

---

(30). I have lately (May 1880) searched again, but still do not find them.

vellers,... 1830.—The new estate, or the young travellers in
Wales and Ireland, by the author of Portugal,... 1831.—
The East Indians at Selwood, or the orphans' home, by the
author of Portugal; the new estate, &c., &c., Lond. Darton
and Harvey, 1834, small 12o.—Gleanings from many fields,
by the author of Portugal, the new estate, &c., &c., Lond.,
Darton and Harvey, 1834, 12o.

Sometimes it is possible to make a tolerably certain guess
at the author, from the similarity in style, or some trick of
the author, as in the punctuation, or the use of italics, as by
Archbishop Whately, or the constant use of the dash, as in
the works of James Flamank.

But in all cases corroborative evidence is necessary. For
how wrong a guess of this kind may be has been amply illustrated in Notes and Queries.

Every celebrated man has had numerous publications at-
tributed to him by people who professed themselves quite
certain of the authorship, from the style and subject matter.

There is at present no book which will give any help in
an investigation like the present. In the "Handbook of
Fictitious Names," at pages 7 and 8, only seven real names
of ladies are revealed, with a note to the effect that there
were upwards of fifty works unknown.

The very useful series of catalogues published by Messrs.
Bent, Hodgson, and Sampson Low, the English Catalogue of
the latter being the best of the kind, afford great assistance.

The London catalogue of books, 1814—1851, has a classified index, and in this anonymous works are frequently at-
tributed to their real authors, though without any indication
of their anonymity.

The British catalogue also has a subject index.

The following include the majority of publications from
1800 to the present time, except pamphlets and privately
printed works.

The London catalogue of books ... since the year 1800 to
March 1827, Lond. pub. for the executor of the late W.
Bent by Longman &c. 1827, 8o.

The London catalogue ... 1814 to 1846.

The London catalogue ... 1816 to 1851, Lond., Thomas
Hodgson 13 Paternoster row and sold by Longman &c.,
1851, 8o.

The classified index to the London catalogue...1816 to
1851, London T. Hodgson 1853, 8o.

The British catalogue of books published from oct. 1837, to dec. 1852 ... by Sampson Low, vol. 1. general alphabet, Lond. S. Low & son, 1853.

In this the dates of publication were added for the first time. The author published an Index to the above in 1858, in which he acknowledges the assistance of Dr. Crestadoro.

The English catalogue of books, published from january, 1835, to january, 1863, comprising the contents of the "London" and the "British" catalogues, and the principal works published in the United States of America and Continental Europe ... compiled by Sampson Low [and assistants], London, S. Low Son & Marston, 1864, r. 8o. And continuations to the present time. So that we thus have names of authors and index of subjects from 1814 to the present time. For the years from 1800 to 1814, Watt's Bibliotheca Britannica can be referred to.

I will now give an illustration.

Information we will say, for example, is sent to the following effect :—

"Sir,—Seeing that you are collecting, with a view to publication, names of authors of the nineteenth century, I beg to say that I was well acquainted with Miss Seaman, who died about the year 1830, a notice of whom you will find in the Ryde papers. She wrote 'Some Observations on Girl's Schools and Boarding Schools,' but whether with her name or not I forget. Also, about 1822, was published, by Smith of London, an interesting religious tale called Lily, and in 16o, 1825, a capital little work on the choice of books, with advice about Miss Edgeworth's Novels."

It will be evident to anyone that the whole of the above requires verification, a labour of hours, perhaps days, which might have been saved by a little bibliographical knowledge on the part of our informant.

On investigation it appears, then, that our informant has scarcely given a single date or title correctly.—1. Miss Seaman died in 1829, not 1830.—2. The reference to the Ryde papers is useless, as too wide for verification, and inaccessible. —3. The title of each of her works is given from recollection, or rather, from no recollection, and they are all incorrect.—4. The titles are made up.—5. Words not in the title-pages are interpolated without notice.—6. The size of the book is placed before the date—i.e. it is interpolated, and in fact everything is reversed.

The above information might be best put in this form.

SEAMAN (Lucy) the daughter of a Captain in the Royal Navy, born at Ryde, the 23 May, 1801, wrote several works which are held in high estimation, and died of consumption on the 15 September, 1829. The following are the only publications I know of from her pen ; but as she published without giving her name, there are probably others that are unknown.

(1) Remarks on education, as at present conducted, especially with reference to private tuition and the system of boarding schools for young ladies, London (printed at Ryde), for the author, 1822, 12mo, pp. iv. 33, anon.

The authoress says, that her father's early death making her, while very young, acquainted with the routine of teaching, was the cause of her publishing these remarks.

(2.) Little Lily, a moral tale for children, by a lady, author of Remarks, &c., Lond. J. Smith, 1823, 8o, pp. 115, 2s 6d, pseudon.

This is the first edition of this excellent little book, the second and subsequent editions of which were published with her name.

We observe that a book entitled " Little Lily's travels, Lond. Nelson, 1860," has been published ; but it is a different work to the above.

(3.) Miss Maria Edgeworth's tales compared with other works of fiction ; to which is added advice for the selection, and a list of works most suitable for children, by the author of Little Lily, &c., Lond., J. Smith, 1826 [1825], 18o, pp. xi and 200, 3s, auton.

In this she complains of her failing health, and expresses her great respect for the writings of her friend Miss Edgeworth.

Here it will be observed that the first work is strictly anonymous, as the abbreviation " anon," indicates, that is to say, it has no name on the title-page, nor any name, pseudonym, nor initials to the preface ; and has in fact no clue whatever as to who is the author, as the reference to her in the imprint cannot be considered such. But from the book being printed at Ryde for the author, though published in London, it may be inferred that she resided at Ryde at the time.

The second work is pseudonymous, as the abbreviation " pseudon," indicates.

The third work would appear also by the title-page to be

pseudonymous, it is not so, as the preface is signed by the authoress, and the abbreviation "auton," warns us that it is autonymous.

In conclusion, I hope that my observations will not dishearten the student who is ambitious of being bibliographical. Let every one strive to do his best. But let no man suppose he can make a good catalogue simply from his desire to do so and without previous study. It is no use saying a man must be accurate, he cannot until he has studied the art of bibliography, and learned what has already been done in that science ; so that by taking note of the errors of his predecessors, he may attempt a catalogue on the most modern and improved principles, and thereby contribute towards the advancement and improvement of bibliography.

———

"Bibliography is a dry occupation,—a caput mortuum,—it is a borrowed production, which brings very little grist to the mill ; and so difficult and tedious is the object, of laying before our eyes all the real or reported copies or editions of the works enumerated, that almost every line of our reports may be suspected of falsehood."—James Atkinson, Medical Bibliography, 1834, 8o [he stopped with letter B].

It is probable that every great national library contains more works without authors' names than with them   Of these anonymous books, a considerable proportion will, doubtless, belong to authors whose names are either known to, or conjectured, more or less plausibly, by the learned bibliographer.   But if conjecture be allowed to govern the *place* of a book in a catalogue, all reliability on it ceases. —Edward Edwards, in the Encyclopædia Britannica, eighth edition, 1857, Art. Libraries, p. 378.

1.   An account of the celebration of the jubilee, on the 25th oct. 1809, being the 49th anniversary of the reign of Geo. III.... collected and published by a lady. Birmingham [1809], 4o.

I should observe that I have not, out of regard to space, put in the pagination, price, &c., and that nearly all the places of publication are abbreviated.   I have seen every book which I here describe, mostly in the Library of the British Museum.

2.   Ailzie Grierson... by a lady. Edin. Johnstone 1846, 16o.

3.   Almeda, or the Neapolitan revenge, a tragic drama, by a lady. Lond. Symonds 1801, 8o.

This is in five acts and in verse.   The advertisement states that part of the plot, which relates to the revenge of the Countess (Almeda) was taken from the " Life of Rozelli."—The author's name was not known to the editors of the Biographia Dramatica 1812.

4.   An alphabet of animals, by a lady. Lond. 1865.

5.   An anecdotal memoir of the princess royal of England from her birth to her marriage [with prince Frederick William of Prussia] by a lady. Lond. Houlston 1858, small 12o.

Prefixed are some verses signed "Mary Bennett."

6. Anecdotes of animals selected by a lady for the amusement of her children. Lond. Darton and Harvey 1832, square 16o.

7. An appeal to the women of England to discourage the stage, by a lady. Lond. Joseph Masters 1855, 24o.

8. The arithmetical class-book, or preparatory studies in arithmetic, by a lady ; for the use of schools, and particularly designed as an assistant for female teachers. Lond. Harvey and Darton 1824, 12o, pp. IV. 62.

> In the preface, dated from "Clapham road place," the authoress says she has had long experience. This little work is not mentioned by De Morgan in his list of Arithmetical books.

9. The Astrologer, a' legend of the Black Forest, by a lady [motto] in two volumes. Lond. Saunders & Otley 1846.

10. The beauties of scripture history for the use of young persons learning English, by a lady. Paris, Ch. Duniol, 29 rue de Tournon 1855.

11. Beauty, what it is, and how to retain it, by a lady : a companion volume to [but not by the authoress of] How to dress on £15 a year... Lond. Warne [1873] 12o.

12. The book of costumes, or annals of fashion... by a lady of rank, illustrated... new edit. Lond. Colburn 1847.

13. The boy's own text book, containing a text from the old and new Testaments... selected by a lady [motto] Lond. J. F. Shaw 1857.

> I need scarcely say that this has nothing in common with "The Boys' Own Book," as to which I had a note in "Notes & Queries" of 27 April, 1878, p. 329. See no. 71.

14. A brief guide to happiness [through religion] by a lady, 2nd edit. revised. Lond. Hope & Co. 1851.

15. Buds and blossoms, or stories of children, by a lady. Lond. Hatchard [1842 ?]. The same work, only anonymous, was also published by Groombridge 1852.

16. Caroline and her mother... principally upon entomological subjects, by a lady [mottoes] Lond. Hatchard 1827.

17. Catechism for the use of young people [motto] by a lady. Paris, published by Galignani 1834.

18. A catechism of the history of England, by a lady. Lond. Dolman 1850.

> One of a series called Dolman's [Catholic] catechisms. The history of France and Germany in the same series are written by A. M. S., and are attributed, with a query, at the British Museum, to Agnes M. Stewart.

19. Cato, or interesting adventures of a dog, interspersed with real anecdotes, by a lady, author of Infant's friend—Easy rhymes, &c. [motto] 3rd edition. Lond. J. Harris, St. Pauls' churchyard [1820 ?] 12o, pp. 175.

> Dedicated to "my little girl," by her mother. "Easy rhymes" appears to be the only one of the above three works in the London Catalogue.

20. The child's guide to knowledge... by a lady. Tho 2nd edit. 1828, the 39th edit. Lond. Simpkin, 1866.

21. The child's manual of prayer, by a lady ... Lond. Dolman 1849. Approved ✝ by Nicholas, bishop of Melipotamus.

22. The child's own book on New-church doctrine, by a lady. Lond. 1837.

23. The child's pathway through the history of England, by a lady, second edition. Lond. Jarrold (Norwich printed) [1858 ?]

The preface is signed Ida, Nottingham, 1855, and I think it may safely be assumed that the authoress lived there.

24. The child's treasure, or reading without spelling effectually simplified... by a lady. Lond. C. H. Law, 1851.

25. Choice descriptive poetry... selected by a lady. Lond. Whittaker, Birmingham (printed) [1852].

26. Chollerton... by a lady. Lond. Ollivier 1846, 8o, pp. 381.

27. The christian's daily preacher... by a lady [motto] Weymouth, 1826.

28. Christmas 1846 and the new year 1847 in Ireland, letters from a lady ; edited by W. S. Gilly... price one shilling : the proceeds of the sale to be given towards relieving the distress in Ireland. Durham, Andrews, 1847, 12o.

"A lady," not wishing her name published, the editor puts his as a guarantee of good faith.

29. A compendium of ancient geography, compiled for the young princess M. L. B*N*P**TE de M——T, intended as a sequel to the abbé Gaultier's excellent Modern geography, as a companion to "Tales of the Classics," and inscribed to governesses ... by a lady. Lond. Hailes, 1835.

30. A compendium of British geography, with questions, by a lady, the author of First lessons in geography. Lond. Hailes 1828(?)

31. Compendium of universal history, by the author of 1000 questions on the old and new Testaments. Lond. Jarrold 1844.

In both the London and English Catalogues, said to be by "a lady," but those words do not occur on the title.

32. Conversations on important scriptural subjects by, a lady. Lond. Ford, Islington 1837, 16o, pp. 102.

33. Conversations on the lord's prayer, by a lady [motto] Lond. Simpkin—Benson and Barling. Weymouth [1851 ?]

The illustration is signed E. J. P.

34. Cookery made easy, by a lady [1841 ?] 11 edit. 1854.

We have from this author : Cheap, nice, and nourishing cookery, or how working people may live well upon a small income...by the author of "Cookery made easy." Lond. Dean [1841].

35. The cottage home... by a lady. Lond. [1864].

36. The cottager's assistant, or the wedding present, 2nd edit., ...by a lady, price 2s. 6d. with plates. Lond. Rodwell & Martin 1824, 12o, pp. VIII. & 47.

Inscribed to the Viscountess Cremorne.

37. A course of... prayers... selected by a lady. Lond. Lyntot, price 2s. 6d., 1804, 8o.

38. Consin Rachel's visit, by a lady. Wellington, Salop, printed by and for Houlston, London 1827.

39. The Cousins, being amusing and instructive lessons in the French language, 2 parts. Lond. Derby, printed [1850].

40. Craigh-Melrose priory ; or memoirs of the Mount Linton family, a novel in four vols, by a lady. Lond. Chapple 1815.

41. The crucifixion, a poem... by a lady. Lond. Cadell 1817.

42. Daily bread, or a text of scripture... selected by a lady. 2nd edit.... Liverpool 1821.

The same published by Seeley, Lond. and Grapel, Liverpool, 1840.

43. Dartmoor legends and other poems, by a lady. Exeter, Roberts 1857.

Dedicated to her father's friend Arthur Howe Holdsworth.

44. Dates of the kings of England, in easy triplets, by a lady Lond. [1874].

45. Domestic economy and cookery, for rich and poor... English, Scotch, French, Oriental and other foreign dishes... by a lady. Lond. John Murray 1827, 12o.

Several editions to the present time, and if not the first, at all events one of the earliest was published by Longmans.

46. An earnest address to young communicants, by a lady. Lond. Rivingtons 1865.

Dedicated by permission to the bishop of Oxford.

47. Easy and familiar sermons for children, by a lady. Lond. printed for the author, Crew and Spencer, 27 Lamb's conduit street and Simpkin and Marshall 1830.

48. Easy lessons in the history of England, by a lady, third edit. Lond. Harvey & Darton 1839.

49. Easy questions and answers from the Pentateuch... by a lady [1855].

50. Economical cookery for young housekeepers...by a lady. Lond. 1824, 4th edit. R. Clarke 1839.

51. Educational outlines and other letters on practical duties, to which is added a journal of a summer's excursion made by the author and her pupils, by a lady. Lond. Groombridge 1850, 8o, pp. 8 and 116, with an illustration of Versailles.

52. Edward Beaumont, or the efficacy of prayer, a narrative founded on facts, by a lady. [motto] Dublin, S. B. Oldham,— Whittaker, Lond. 1844.

53. Ellie's and the Doctor's tales... by a lady, with (five) illustrations by the same. Lond. Darton [1859]

54. Eight days' journey to Matlock, by a lady. Wakefield, printed for John Robinson, Express Office 1860.

55. An elementary compendium of music for the use of schools, by a lady. Lond. John Murray 1835, quarto, pp. VII. and 72, price 12s.

56. Emily Trevor, or the Vale of Elwy, by a lady. Lond. Simpkin, Denbigh (printed by) T. Gee 1850.

This is inscribed to Mrs. Maconochie of Meadow-bank house.

57. English history, in the way of question and answer, by a lady, new edit. Lond. [1839 ?].

58. The English mother, or early lessons on the church of England, by a lady [mottoes] Bath (printed) W. Pocock. Lond. Simpkin 1840, 8o, pp. xii, 84 : list of subscribers.

59. Enquiries for the truth between the divided church militant denominated Roman and Protestant, by a lady. Canterbury (printed by) Henry Ward. Lond. Hatchard 1851.

60. Esthwaite water, a poem in three parts... by a lady. Lond. Whittaker : Kendal (printed by) J. Hudson 1854, 8o, pp. 44, with an engraving signed W. Banks, sc. Edin.

61. Every lady her own cook ; or a few practical hints as to how the patent Crimean cooking stove can be used to the best advantage, by a lady. Dublin, McGlashan 1857.

62. Every lady's guide to her own greenhouse... by a lady. Lond. Orr 1851.

63. An explanation of the ten commandments, by a lady ; revised by a clergyman of the church of England. Lond. Tabart 1802, small 12o, pp. 40.

64. An explanation of the two sacraments and the occasional rites and ceremonies of the church of England, in a series of dialogues between a mother (Mrs. Vernon) and her daughters (Louisa and Mary) intended for the use of young persons. Lond. John Murray 1828, 8o. pp. XI. and 1 and 271.

Inscribed to Mr. Justice Parke.

As catalogued by Lowndes in the "British Librarian," p. 782, this little work well illustrates some of my previous observations. Lowndes gives part of the title, and afterwards puts a note in the words of the rest of the title. His date is later than mine. but he does not say it is a new edition. The following is a copy of Lowndes' entry :—"629. An Explanation of the Two Sacraments and the occasional Rites and Ceremonies of the Church of England, by a Lady, London, 1831, sm. 8vo, publ. at 5s. 6d. A series of dialogues between a mother and her daughters, intended for the use of young persons."

65. Extracts of letters to a christian friend, by a lady, with an introductory essay by Thos. Erskine, esq., advocate, author of "Remarks on the internal evidences for the truth of revealed religion," etc., etc. R. B. Lusk Greenock. Glasgow 1830.

66. Familiar dialogues, on interesting subjects... by a lady. Lond. Rivington 1821.

It might occur to any one that the publishers would give the author's name, my enquiries from this source were so constantly and uniformly unsuccessful that I never resort to publishers now.

67. Flora and Thalia, or germs of flowers and poetry; being an alphabetical arrangement of flowers, with appropriate poetical illustrations [selected from various authors] embellished with coloured plates (M. Spratt del.): by a lady [motto] Lond. Washbourne 1835, small 12o, pp. XII. 200.

Dedicated by permission to the duchess of Kent and the princess Victoria. The preface is addressed from "King's road Chelsea."

68. Florence Nightingale and the Russian war, a poem, by a lady. Lond. Hatchard 1856.

The authoress says "she had the honour of being nearly connected with one of the greatest naval commanders of the age in which he lived."

69. Footprints for little christians, by a lady, price sixpence. Salisbury. Lond. Simpkin [1860].

70. Garden of language [motto] London, Fisher son & co. Newgate street 1835, 16o, pp. 31, with illustrations.

This is a sort of English grammar, and is said in the London Catalogue to be by a lady.

71. The girls' own text book, containing a text... for every morning and evening in the year: selected by a lady. Lond. J. F. Shaw 1858, 32o, see no 13.

72. Glimpses of natural history, by a lady [motto] London, Darton & Harvey (1843) [afterwards bought by R. Clarke] square 16o, pp. VI. 199, with illustrations, some signed J. B.

73. A glimpse of Oriental Nature, pictures with verses by a lady, with a preface by... G. R. Gleig. Lond. Dean & Son 1865, 4o.

74. Grandmamma's first catechism, by a lady, second edition. Oxford (printed) and London, J. H. Parker 1854, 24o, pp. 23.

75. "Guess if you can" ! a collection of enigmas and charades in verse, together with 50 in the French language, by a lady. Lond. Bogue 1851, 8o.

76. A guide for the sick chamber, consisting of prayers, hymns and portions of scripture selected... by a lady. Edinburgh 1837, 12o.

77. Harp of Salem, a collection of historical poems from the scriptures, together with some reflective pieces, by a lady. Edinb. James Taylor, Smith & co. Hunter square 1827, 12o, pp. V. 224.

78.   The history of David the King of Israel, in two parts, by a lady [motto] London, printed by H. Teape, Tower hill, sold by Blanchard, City road ; Kent, Hamilton ; and Keene, Dublin 1817, 12o, pp. 4 and 184.

The advertisement states that this was originally written for the Youths Magazine, and that the first part appeared in the tenth volume of that publication.

79.   The home book, or young housekeeper's assistant, forming a complete system of domestic economy and household accounts, with estimates of expenditure, &c., &c., in every department of housekeeping founded on forty-five years' experience, by a lady [motto] London, Smith, Elder & co. 1829, 12o, pp. VII. 175.

Starts upon the assumption that the lady's husband has not less than £1000 a year.

80.   Hours with the Leslies, a tale for children, and Phantasie's birthday, a fairy tale, by a lady. London, Hope & co. 16 Great Marlborough street 1853 [1852] large 16o, pp. 4 and 200.

81.   How to dress on £15 a year as a lady, by a lady [Mrs. Millicent Whiteside Cook] Lond. Warne 1873.

This little work was the subject of a Chancery suit, Warne the original publisher against Routledge, the publisher of a second edition before Warne's was exhausted. Mrs. Cook's royalty was one penny per copy sold, and Warne very shortly paid her £100.—See Law Reports. Master of the Rolls 12 June 1874 xviii. 497.

82.   Hymns and thoughts for the sick and lonely, by a lady. London. Nisbet [Bath 1848] 12o.

New edition Nisbet 1859.

83.   Hymns for times of sickness and sorrow selected from various authors by a lady, the profits of the work will be given to the Cholera orphan home, Ham Common near Richmond... London, Wertheim and Macintosh 24 Paternoster row [1849] small 12o, pp. 34.

Inscribed to rev. Joseph Brown, rector of Christ church, Surrey, dated from Keythorpe Hall.

84.   Ines, and other poems [motto] London, printed for Allman 1816, 8o, pp. 4 and 208.

The London Catalogue says this is by a lady, but those words do not occur on the title.

85.   Jesus the Messiah, or the Old testament prophecies fulfilled in the New testament scriptures, by a lady, the profits to be devoted to charitable purposes. London, Seeley and Burnside 1822, 12o, pp. XIX. 264.

Dedicated to the right rev. Charles Richard lord bishop of Winchester.

86.   The juvenile gardener written by a lady, for the use of her own children, with a view of giving them an early taste for the pleasures of a garden and the study of botany [motto] Lond. printed for Harvey and Darton and sold by John Rodford, Hull 1824, 12o, pp. 126.

87.   Kaisersworth Deaconesses, including a history of the Institution : the ordination service and questions for self examination, by a lady. Lond. Masters 1857, 12o.

88.   The ladies' guide to life assurance : briefly shewing the necessity for its more extended practice amongst the female community, by a lady. Lond. Partridge, Oakey & co. 34 Paternoster row 1854, 18o, pp. 32.

It is dedicated by permission to the duchess of Hamilton and Brandon. The preface is signed J. B. and dated Greenwich 24 Nov. 1854.

89.   The lady's guide to the ordering of her household and the economy of the dinner table, by a lady. London, Smith & Elder 1861, 8o, pp. XVI. 500.

90.   Letters on confirmation, a manual of moral and religious duties, designed for the young of her own sex in the upper ranks of society, by a lady. London, Cleaver 1846, 16o.

91.   Letters to my unknown friends, by a lady. Lond. printed of for Longman, &c. 1846, 8o, pp. VI. 294 ; also 1849 and 1853.

Also author of Some passages in Modern history.

92.   The life of Mary, mother of our Lord... by a lady. Lond 1851, 8o.

93.   Lilias, or fellowship with God...by a lady [with an introduction by...C. B. Tayler] Edin. 1859, 8o.

94.   Lines addressed to prince Leopold of Saxe-Cobourg on the death of his consort the princess Charlotte of Wales, by a lady. Colchester, printed and sold by Swinborne and Walter; Hatchard, London 1817, 8o, pp. 7.

95.   Little Christian's sunday alphabet, by a lady, woodcuts. 1849, 16o.

96.   Mandeville, or the Lynmouth visitors, Barnstaple printed by Brightwell & son, sold also by Longman & co., Whittaker & co., Lond.; Roberts, Exeter; Nettleton, Plymouth 1839, 8o, pp. VII. 164.

97.   Mary Queen of Scots, an historical ballad with other poems by a lady. Lond. printed for John Stockdale, Piccadilly 1800, 16o, pp. 89, 2s. 6d.

98.   Method for teaching plain needlework in schools, by a lady (second edition). London, Robert Hardwicke 192 Piccadilly [1861] 8o.

The title page is lithographed. The preface is signed M. E. B., Decr. 1861. I have not seen the first edition of 1857. The authoress says she received her information thirty years before 1861.

99.   Metrical remembrances, by a lady [motto from Isaiah xl. 29] London 1832, 16o.

No publisher's name, S. Bagster, Junr. printer.

100.   Modern household cookery, a new work for private families, by a lady, with an introduction on the philosophy of cookery. London, Nelson 1860, 8o, pp. XV. 396, and plates.

48 LIST OF WORKS BY A LADY.

101. The modern cookery, written upon the most approved
and economical principles, and in which every receipt has stood
the test of experience, by a lady, second edition, with considerable
additions by the author. Derby, printed by and for Henry Mozley
1820, 12o.

102. Murray's modern cookery book. Modern domestic cookery
based on the well-known works of Mrs. Rundell, but including all
the recent improvements in the culinary art: founded on principles of economy and practical knowledge and adapted for private
families, by a lady, with illustrative woodcuts. Lond. John Murray 1851, 8o, xxviii. 675.

> "The arrangement of the whole work, previously enriched with the
> valuable contributions of the late Miss Emma Roberts (whose receipts
> are marked E. R.) has been placed under the careful inspection of
> a lady well versed in the art of which it treats. The book has had
> the further advantage of being thoroughly revised by a professional
> gentleman of great repute in London, who has also supplied several
> valuable receipts."—Preface.

103. Moral maxims from the wisdom of Jesus the son of Sirach,
or the Ecclesiasticus, selected by a lady, and enriched with six
engravings from drawings of her own. Lond. Harris 1807.

104. My Norske note book ; or a month in Norway, by a lady.
Lond. Westerton 1860 [1859] 8o.

105. Natural history of quadrupeds, for children... by a lady,
2nd edit., with plates. Lond. Harvey and Darton 1824, 12o, 4s.
3rd edit. 182—?

106. The new estate, or the young travellers in Wales and
Ireland, by author of Portugal, &c. Lond. printed for Darton and
Harvey 1831, 12o, pp. vii. 302, with illustrations.

> The same names and persons occur in "The young travellers in Portu-
> gal." The authoress acknowledges having availed herself of a small
> work called "Fairy Legends" [by Croker] in speaking of popular
> superstitions. The "New Estate" is in Ireland.

107. The Orb of light ; or the Apocalyptic vision (with the
text of the Revelation) by a lady. Lond. Wertheim, 1860, 8o.

108. Original fables [in verse] by a lady ; dedicated to her
royal highness the princess Charlotte of Wales, embellished with
fifty-four elegant engravings on wood. Lond. printed for B. Crosby
& co. 1810 ; 12o, other editions 1812 and 1815.

109. Outlines of truth by a lady. London, Hatchard 1825, 12o.

110. The philanthropist, or selfishness and benevolence illustrated : a tale, by a lady [mottoes] London, Wm. Ball 1836, 8o,
pp. vi. 389.

> Announced as by the same author 'The spirit of sectarianism,' 8o,
> pp. 75, 1s. 6d. This is a different work to the Philanthropist by
> P. S. Goss.

111. Plain lectures on Genesis for family reading, by a lady.
Lond. Pickering 1841, 8o.

112. Poems for children, by a lady. Lond. Darton and Harvey 1834, 12o, pp. IV. 66.

113. A poetical picture of America, being observations made during a residence of several years at Alexandria and Norfolk in Virginia...1799 to 1807, by a lady. London, printed for the author and sold by Vernor Hood & Sharpe 31 Poultry 1809, small 8o, pp. 14 and 177.

W. Wilson, printer, St. John's square. It has a list of subscribers.

114. Portions of Scripture, with... a view to promote the observance of the Lord's day, by a lady. Lond. J. Hatchard & Son 1837, price 3d, or 2s 6d a dozen, 12o, pp. 12.

115. Portugal, or the young travellers, being some account of Lisbon and its environs, and of a tour in the Alemtéjo ; from a journal kept by a lady during three years' actual residence. Lond. Darton & Harvey 1830, 12o.

116. Private memoirs of the Court of Louis XVIII. by a lady, 2 vols Lond. Colburn 1830, 8o.

117. Prayers, hymns, and texts, by a lady. Lond. Seeley 1846, 12o.

118. Ravensdale, a tale by a lady [of Dublin] 2 vols. Dublin, Curry & co. ; Lond. Longman 1845, 12o.

119. Recollections of a seven years' residence at the Mauritius or Isle of France, by a lady. London, James Cawthorn 1830, 8o, pp. XI. 208.

The work is dedicated to Ellen & Mary. The preface is signed by their "Mother." She speaks of her daughters as orphans.

120. The Redeemed Rose, or Willies rest, by a lady. Lond. 1853, 8o.

121. A residence at Sierra Leone, described from a journal kept on the spot and from letters written to friends at home, by a lady [edited by the Hon. C. E. S. Norton] Lond. 1849, 16o.

One of Murray's Home and Colonial Library.

122. The restoration of the works of art to Italy, a poem by a lady [motto] Oxford, printed by W. Baxter for R. Pearson High street, Oxford, and J. Ebers, Old Bond street, London 1816, 8o, pp. 23.

123. Return to my native village ; and other poems chiefly on sacred subjects, by a lady. Oxford and Lond. Parker 1853, 16o.

124. The Rev. Jabez Bunting, or begging ; with other poems by a lady, printed at the request of friends of the authoress. William Illingworth, printer, top of Kirkgate, Leeds 1833; entered at Stationers' Hall, 12o, pp. 14.

125. The rich old bachelor, a domestic tale [in verse] in the style of Dr. Syntax [by W. Combe] by a lady [motto] Ward, Printer, Canterbury 1824, 8o, pp. 312.

126. The Sceptic, by a lady. Lond. J. Russell Smith 1850, 8o, pp. VIII. 168.

Crewkerne (Somersetshire) printed by G. P. R. Pulman, Market-place.

127. A scriptural guide to the duties of every-day life... compiled by a lady. Lond. Saunders and Otley 1846, 12o.

128. Selina, a novel, founded on facts, by a lady, in three volumes.

—— Is there not a hand,
Which operates unseen, and regulates
The vast machine we tread on? Dr. Hurdis.

Lond. printed for C. Law Ave maria lane, by Bye and Law, St. John's-square, Clerkenwell 1800, 12o.

The authoress's first work.

129. A series of reflections on the sacred oratorio of the Messiah [by Handel] by a lady. London, Hatchard 1812, 8o.

For full title see the British Critic, XL. 201.

130. The siege of Mansoul a drama in five acts [and in verse] the diction of which consists altogether in an accommodation of words from Shakespeare and other poets, by a lady [motto] Bristol, sold by W. Bulgin No. 3 Wine street, sold also by Matthews, strand. Longman, &c., Lond.; and S. Hazard, Bath 1801, 8o, VI. 82.

"The composition of a lady now deceased." Part of the preface is written by the Rev. H. Sulger. It is not in Baker's Biog. Dramatica, 1812.

131. Sketch of ancient geography, by a lady for the use of her own pupils. Brighton & Lond. Whittaker 1857, 8o.

132. Spain yesterday and to-day, by a lady. Lond. Harvey & Darton [1829] sm. 8o.

133. The stepping stone to astronomy, by a lady. Longmans 1858, 16o.

134. Suspirium sanctorum, or holy breathings, a series of prayers for every day in the month, by a lady. Lond. Saunders & Otley 1826, 8o.

135. Tales from the German, by a lady. Lond. Anderson [1825?] 8o.

136. Tales of the classics, a new delineation of the most popular fables, legends and allegories commemorated in the works of poets, painters and sculptors, selected and written by a lady for the amusement and instruction of her own daughters [mottoes] in three volumes. London, Colburn and Bentley, 1830, 12o, vol I. XXIV. 302, vol. II. IV. 302, vol III. 370 the pagination of the appendix is continuous.

Dedicated to H.R.H. the princess Victoria of Kent, dated from "Wadlands," July 1829.

137. A text book [religious] for the sick and afflicted, selected by a lady. Lond. J. F. Shaw 1858, 16o.

138.' Tales original and translated from the Spanish, by a lady, embellished with eight engravings on wood. London J. J. Stockdale, 41 Pall Mall 1810, 8o, pp. 391.

Dedicated by the publisher to Anna Eliza Chandos, Countess Temple The advertisement dated from Whitchurch, Hampshire, states that these are the production of a young lady unknown in the metropolis, and unused to writing for the public.

139. Thoughts on our national calamity in a letter to a friend in Ireland, by a lady [motto] London, Rivington 1817, 8o, pp. 66.

On the death of the princess Charlotte Augusta of Wales.

140. Translations and sketches of biography from the German, Italian, Spanish, Portuguese, and French languages, by a lady. Lond. Saunders & Otley 1839, 8o.

141. Twelve years a go, a tale, by [a lady] the author of Letters to unknown friends. Lond. Longman 1847, 16o.

142. Twice Married, my own story, by a lady. Lond. Ward & Lock 1855, 8o.

143. Two fairy tales in a dramatic form, by a lady [Miss Clode formerly of Wooton under Edge ?] Lond. A. Hall 1851, 12o.

144. Variety, a collection of original poems, by a lady. London, printed by J. Davison, White-friars, for James Wallis, Paternoster row, and Christopher and Jennet, Stockton 1802, small 8o, pp. VIII., 167 and 1.

145. "Vater Unser," a tale for children, illustrative of the Lord's prayer, translated freely from the German, by a lady. Lond. Whittaker & Co. 1844, 12o, pp. 48.

Dedicated to A**** M***** B******, a child of seven years old, by her mother.

146. Village incidents, or religious influence in domestic scenes by a lady. London, Hatchard 1828, 12o, pp. VIII. 145.

147. Woman as a virgin, wife, and mother, by a lady. Lond. Mitchell [1838] 16o, 1s. 6d.

148. A word in favor of female schools, addressed to parents guardians and the public at large, by a lady [motto] London, Longman 1826, 24o, pp. 74, 2s. 6d.

149. Workwoman's guide ; containing instructions in cutting out and completing those articles of wearing apparel, etc., which are actually made at home, etc. Lond. Simpkin, Birmingham, print. 1838, 4to.

New edit. Simpkin 1840, 4to, 21s.

150. Ward's illustrated geography in question and answer, a sequel to "First lessons in geography by a lady." Lond. Ward [Bungay printed 1853] 12o, 4 edit. 1859.

151. The young lady's friend, by a lady. Glasgow, W. R. Mc Phun 1857, 16o, pp. 128.

A book of advice and etiquette. The English catalogue 1835—1862 p. 855 gives a work with this title published by Parker & son 1852.

A few words on Swimming, with practical hints, by R. Harrington ; to which is added a bibliographical list of works on swimming by Olphar Hamst. Price one shilling.

> I had a few thick paper copies of the list struck off separately with the following title :—
>
> Swimming : a bibliographical list of works on swimming, by the author of the handbook of fictitious names, 1868.
>
> I put the word " Swimming " at the head and used a phrase for pseudonym, so that it might be catalogued under the subject at the British Museum instead of being buried under my name.

Catalogue of the Etchings and Drypoints of J. A. M. Whistler. 1874, with an etching by Percy Thomas of Whistler, after a portrait by himself. Only fifty copies printed. One guinea each.

INDEX.

(*Pub.* = *Publisher.*)